RABBIT AND THE MOTORBIKE

by Kate Hoefler   art by Sarah Jacoby

chronicle books · san francisco

Rabbit lived in a quiet field of wheat that he never left—not even once—even though there was a road. And even though he dreamed he did every night.

Every night.

But Dog would visit.

Dog was too old and sick to leave the field now, but he had
spent most of his life going all over the country on his motorbike,

and he loved telling Rabbit about the places he'd felt most alive,

where he'd howled at the moon.

Dog made Rabbit feel that wherever he'd been,
Rabbit had been right there with him.
Rabbit loved Dog.

"The world is beautiful," Dog would say, "if you're brave enough to see it. Even new places can feel like long-lost friends."

Every day was filled with a good story by Dog.

Every day.

Until the day it was filled with a bad one.

And Rabbit's field was quiet again. The days were wheat.

Except for one day, when he heard a not-quiet sound.

Rabbit didn't know why Dog would leave his motorbike to *him*, since he didn't go anywhere.

He hoped the bike would like not going anywhere.

On days Rabbit collected carrots, the motorbike collected leaves.

But not for long. The wind always carried the leaves to faraway places.

When birds made nests in its spokes, there was birdsong.

But it was a life quieter than a bird's. And the birds always left.

One night when Rabbit was in the mood for a story, he brought the motorbike in. But it didn't tell Rabbit any stories, and Rabbit had none to tell it.

So they just listened to the distant sounds of the highway.

When summer came, everything was growing and blooming.
Even the road blossomed out. Rabbit and the motorbike stayed
planted on the porch.

Because I'm scared, he told it one night,
as if it had asked a question.

When Rabbit slept, he heard the long howl of its
engine in his dreams. A beautiful howl.

Okay, he said softly to the bike one afternoon. *Just down the road.*

But roads are long. Rabbit forgot that.

Quite long.

Long roads took him to where the giant
redwoods were—where Rabbit was the
wind that carried the leaves.

And by the sea, where birdsong whirled—   where all the birds wanted to fly like Rabbit.

And through the Mojave Desert, where Rabbit howled at the moon—
where he felt wild and wondrous—

and full of stories.

Wherever they went, Rabbit and the motorbike were
the distant sound of the highway that others heard.

And Rabbit felt Dog right there with him.

The heart can sing like that.

Certain roads take all summer to get back to a field of wheat,
Rabbit noticed. Especially on a motorbike.

But this road eventually did.

And when it did, the days were wheat again.

But they were also motorbike, and wings,

and stories.

Stories that kept old friends—and new—

right there with him.

Library of Congress Cataloging-in-Publication Data

Names: Hoefler, Kate, author. | Jacoby, Sarah (Illustrator), illustrator.

Title: Rabbit and the motorbike / by Kate Hoefler ; illustrated by Sarah Jacoby.

Description: San Francisco, California : Chronicle Books LLC, [2019] | Summary: Rabbit lives, happy and content, in a wheat field, never venturing outside its bounds; but he enjoys old Dog's stories of life on the road with his motorbike— so when Dog dies and leaves Rabbit his bike, Rabbit starts to feel the powerful pull of the open road.

Identifiers: LCCN 2018041273 | ISBN 9781452170909 (alk. paper). Subjects: LCSH: Rabbits—Juvenile fiction. | Dogs—Juvenile fiction. | Motorcycles—Juvenile fiction. | Friendship—Juvenile fiction. | CYAC: Rabbits— Fiction. | Dogs—Fiction. | Motorcycles—Fiction. | Friendship—Fiction. | LCGFT: Picture books. Classification: LCC PZ7.1.H62 Rab 2019 | DDC 813.6 [E] —dc23 LC record available at https://lccn.loc.gov/2018041273

Manufactured in China.

Design by Amelia Mack.

Typeset in Requiem.

The illustrations in this book were rendered in watercolor, NuPastel, and mixed media.

10 9 8 7 6 5 4 3 2 1

Chronicle Books LLC

680 Second Street

San Francisco, California 94107

www.chroniclekids.com

For those who live in me. Thank you.—K. H.

To Dad, may you always dream of big adventures.—S. J.